For William,

my wolf protector.

On top of a hill

sat a little wolf pup

Who lived all alone

with no one to love.

The Little WOLF

By Hilary Yelvington

Illustrated by Vanessa Palacio

MATCHBOX PRESS

With his head on his paws,

he looked down the hill,

At a house warm and cozy,

that shut out the chill.

He dreamed of a
playmate who lived
in the house,

Who cuddled and
played and fed him
stuffed mouse.

3

Then one day he roamed

from the hill he called home

with hopes for a friend

he could call his own.

4

So up to the door of
the little old house,
the pup clambered quickly
in hopes of stuffed mouse.

But the door crashed open

and the pup's blood ran cold,

For in front of him stood a man

who was withered and old.

He walked with a stick and

his pants slouched down,

He was skinny and bent

and his face wore a frown.

"Come here, young pup,"

he said with a growl.

"Come have some milk,"

shook his wrinkly jowls.

The little wolf agreed and inched slowly inside,

then the old man snatched up the pup by his hide.

"Now you're mine," said the man as he searched for a leash.

"I'll keep you with me, my beautiful beast!"

For days, weeks and
months the young
pup lingered on.

Though he was
kept safe and fed,
all his old dreams
were gone.

Of fun with the sweet little friend he adored,

instead he laid here with the man,

cozy but bored.

Then one cold, dark night came a shadowy fiend.

His long fangs were
white and his smooth
scales were green.

13

The creature came closer, then to his surprise,

The pup saw a snake with two shiny red eyes.

At first it looked sharply

upon the young pup,

but then it smiled, hissing,

"Come here,

little cub."

"There's no need to fear,

I'm a viper, you see.

And all that I want is

something to eat."

"I don't eat wolves or

grumpy old men,

my sweet little pup,

could you use a friend?"

"I've been watching you

here as you slump on the floor,

But all hope is not lost,

Let me in through the door!"

"Just let me inside, and please do not yip.

That humbug doesn't like me,

not one little bit."

So in slid the
viper to search
for some food,
but the little wolf
could tell he was up
to no good.

He yelped for the man
who was dozing inside.

The viper hissed, "Quiet!" and bared his fangs wide.

Then in his
big boots,
the old man
came running,

The viper slipped past him,
quick, mean and cunning.

The pup shrank back in
the shadows and shook,
as he watched the old man
catch the snake with a hook.

It slithered and snapped as
the man gripped its tail,

but the viper slid free
and made the man wail.

19

"I've been bit!" screamed the man,
and he fell to the ground.

The viper snuck off without making a sound.

The little wolf crept forth
and looked down
at the man,

Who reached up
to the pup with
a wrinkly old hand.

"I'm sorry, my boy, for keeping you here.

I've been all alone for so many years.

But I'm happy I'm not on my own at the end,

for you're here with me, my very good friend."

As the man closed his eyes, all at once it was clear,

the love the pup longed for was lying right here!

"Help!"

he barked.

And he started to run,

up the road to the village

to look for someone.

At last on the road he

saw someone standing,

he bounded right up to her,

huffing and panting.

Then he tugged on the cuff
of her pants til she followed,
to help the old man, whose
breathing grew shallow.

"Oh my,"

she said when she saw him there lying,

"I'll suck out the poison to keep him from dying!"

25

She did as she promised,

then put him to bed,

For three days
he laid there,
resting his head.

At last he sat up
and opened his eyes.
He found Doctor Denise,
So caring and wise,

And the little wolf
who saved him,
with barks, tugs and cries.

And then tears of joy ran down his old face,

as he cherished his friends in a long, warm embrace.

They visited each day,
those wonderful three,

Eating pie, telling stories
and playing happily.

30

Hilary Yelvington

Hilary started writing stories when she was 7 years old after falling in love with Sherlock Holmes and Agatha Christie mysteries. She's been a newspaper reporter, a researcher, an editor, a ghostwriter and more. After scribbling in notebooks for years, Hilary's two young children inspired her to go pro. She lives in the Chicago suburbs with her family.

Vanessa Palacio

Vanessa is a Colombian illustrator and graphic designer. Her work is inspired by her love for nature and animals. She lives in the Pacific North West.